Maisy at the Beach
Sticker Book

W9-BDB-703

Lucy Cousins

Take the sticker pages out of the middle of this book.
Open the pages so the stickers and the pictures
in the book can be seen side by side.
Read the words on each page.
Then choose which sticker to peel off
and where to put it in each picture.

CANDLEWICK PRESS

Maisy and her friends
are at the
beach.

Can you put on their sun hats?

Eddie goes swimming. What else is in the water?

It's very
sunny!
Maisy looks
 for seashells
in the sand.

Find Cyril's shovel
and help him build
a sandcastle.

Catch the beach ball, Tallulah!

Find Panda and put him under the palm tree.

Eddie and Charley sail their toy boats.

Charley needs his inner tube.

Cyril and Maisy
buy ice-cream cones.

Find an umbrella for the ice-cream cart.

A day at the beach is lots of fun!
Bye-bye, Maisy.